MW00937393

THE TRAVEL KIDS

BOOK 2

The Rescue of Princess Okalani

Judith Sessler

THE TRAVEL KIDS

BOOK 2

The Rescue of Princess Okalani

copyright 2016 by Judith Sessler

ALL RIGHTS RESERVED. NO PART OF THIS BOOK MAY BE USED WITHOUT WRITTEN PERMISSION OF AUTHOR

ALL CHARACTERS PORTRAYED ARE FICTITIOUS. ANY RESEMBLANCE TO REAL PERSONS LIVING OR DEAD IS PURELY COINCIDENTAL

The Travel Kids Series

BOOK ONE
BOTHERSOME BOBBY AND THE TRAVEL KIDS
copyright 2016 by Judith Sessler

also

BY JUDITH SESSLER

THE WORLD OF AIDAN McMANUS
copyright 2009 by Judith Sessler

SAINTS AND SINNERS
short stories from the bizarre to the sublime
copyright 2016 by Judith Sessler

FIFTY SHADES OF GREEN OR COFFEEHOUSE CONFESSIONS OF THE UNCOMMON JOE
copyright 2016 by Judith Sessler

for Isabella, my little collaborator

ACKNOWLEDGMENT

I thank my family who have supported and encouraged me every step of the way in my writing career

TABLE OF CONTENTS

CHAPTER ONE

"I am *so* glad you're back!"
Heloise said as she hugged Eva.

"So are *we*, Heloise," Henry said.

"We were really scared that we
were going to be lost out there forever,"
Eva said.

"I know it wasn't Bobby and
Amanda's fault that they intercepted us
in that movie theater and broke our
rings, but they certainly caused us a lot
of trouble," Henry said.

"I was really afraid, Heloise. What
would have happened if we couldn't

make it back?" Eva asked.

"It's really better that you don't know," Heloise said gently.

She knew if she told them the truth they might not want to risk traveling ever again.

Heloise was in charge of Henry and Eva. It was her responsibility to send them where they needed to go and to make sure they were safe. When Bobby and Amanda knocked their travel rings out of kilter, she was desperate to find them and get them back safely. They had no idea how close they came to being stranded in the nebula, where they would never be seen again. Heloise would be able to look up into the dark midnight sky and see the luminous cloud and know they were trapped in there for all of eternity.

Yes, it was best they never knew how close they came to disappearing forever.

"So tell me, how were Amanda and Bobby when you left them?" Heloise asked.

"Bobby was so happy he hugged Amanda. I don't think he did much of that before they came with us. I think Bobby might have been a little stinker, but this experience seemed to have straightened him right out," Eva laughed.

"Yes, I thought that might have been the case," Heloise chuckled.

"I don't think he'll be playing any pranks anytime soon...if *ever*," she said.

"When we left, they knew that no

one would ever believe their story, so they have a secret they can share forever," Henry said.

Eva looked over at Henry and smiled. They both had become very fond of Bobby and Amanda and wished they could have remained friends, but they knew that they were travel kids and travel kids just couldn't *have* friends. Their life, their destiny, was to travel wherever Heloise sent them and do whatever they were supposed to do for her.

"Do we get to stay here for a while, or are we on our way again?" Eva asked, hoping they could stay a while.

They loved to travel, but Heloise was such fun and sometimes they just wanted to hang out with her.

"I'm afraid you can only stay a few days and then you have to go again," Heloise said sadly.

She always hated when they left. They didn't know it, but she was very lonely when they were gone. They didn't know that there was no one else for Heloise. Eva and Henry were the only 'family' she had. When they had been in danger of being lost forever with Bobby and Amanda, Heloise cried the whole time, until thcy finally made it home safe and sound.

"When do we have to leave?" Eva asked, sadly.

"Sunday."

It was Thursday so they had three days before they were off again.

"Where are we off to next?"

Henry asked.

"Why don't you kids relax and settle in. We can talk about it Sunday morning," Heloise said as she put a plate a homemade peanut butter cookies on the table.

Uh-oh, Henry thought. Our favorite cookies *and* she's not going to tell us until right before we leave.

He knew that might be an ominous sign. They had traveled to many places and been in many different situations, but only a few of them were really dangerous.

There was just something about the way Heloise was acting that made him think maybe this was going to be one of those times.

Well, no need to worry about it tonight, he thought. He took a cookie and gave it to Eva and then took one for himself.

    We'll find out soon enough.

8

CHAPTER TWO

Sunday morning, Henry woke up just as the sun rose above the horizon. He was always the early riser and Eva would sleep the whole day away if you let her. On travel days he always got up earlier than usual because he wanted to talk to Heloise alone. Sometimes their travels took them to places that were fun and exciting where there wasn't any danger. But then there were a few that were *very* dangerous.

It was Heloise's responsibility to help get them out of trouble, but there were times she wasn't able to and then

Henry had to try and figure out things for himself.

It wasn't always easy. They had some very narrow escapes, like the ones they just came back from. Getting tangled up in time and space with Bobby and Amanda was the scariest of all. Their travel rings were thrown out of whack when they were intercepted and Heloise was unable to help. Henry was afraid they would be lost forever in the nebula.

Heloise never gave him any details about the nebula. It was as if she was afraid to tell him. Henry figured it must be pretty awful if she had to keep it secret. All she told them was that it was a cloud of dust far away in the dark, black sky. Henry was afraid they would fall into a black hole in space and never be seen again.

"Okay, Henry, let's go into the kitchen," Heloise said quietly, so as not to wake Eva.

Henry followed her and they sat down at the table.

Heloise didn't have her usual smiling face on. She seemed serious. Henry suspected this was going to be one of their harder trips.

He must have looked nervous.

"Don't look so worried," Heloise said, "It's not *that* bad."

"Not *that* bad? So that means it's not all that good, either," Henry said, trying to laugh, but not able to.

He wouldn't have minded if it was just him, but he had to look after his younger sister, Eva. She was too young to be aware of the dangers that lurked around them and she often needed to be rescued from some bad situation.

Sometimes they were *really* bad and he couldn't let on just how dangerous it was.

There was the time in 1792 when she was nearly beheaded in the guillotine in France. Then there was the time she was nearly whisked away and drowned in the Great Mississippi flood of 1927. Then there was that time he had to save her from an avalanche in the Alps. Then there was the time...

Heloise interrupted his thoughts.

"Henry!" she said and snapped him back to reality.

"Sorry, Heloise. I was just thinking about..." he said.

"Yes, I know. It's a big responsibility," she said as she tilted her head towards the sleeping Eva.

"You're a really good, big brother. Eva knows how lucky she is," Heloise smiled.

Eva started to stir when she heard her name.

Henry lowered his voice to a whisper.

"You'd better tell me now, before she wakes up. I want time to prepare what to say."

She'll know about it soon enough, he thought to himself.

14

CHAPTER THREE

"There's an island in the South Seas called Tanaka. *Most* of the natives are very friendly, but the ones you will have to watch out for are the... headhunters," Heloise said calmly, so Henry wouldn't yell out 'headhunters??' and wake Eva.

Actually, to Heloise's surprise, he didn't say anything at all.

He just sat there, silently thinking.

"Are you all right, Henry?" she asked.

"I'm not sure, Heloise. We've been in some pretty scary situations before, but not quite this scary," he said quietly.

He was trying not to let his fear show in his voice.

It was true. This was the first time when they could have their heads chopped off, shrunken and hung on a pole. The thought scared him to death.

Well, there was the time with Eva and the guillotine, and he didn't know why, but somehow it didn't seem as bad as this.

Eva started to stir and they knew it was best to just stick to the basics when they told her where they were going. She didn't need to know the gory details of the danger involved.

"Good morning, Eva," Heloise

said. "Did you sleep well?"

Heloise and Henry knew that she always slept well.

"Yup. I'm *hungry*. What's for breakfast?"

"Now you sound like Bobby. He was always saying that, no matter where we traveled to, remember?" Henry chuckled.

"Yeah, he did," she laughed.

Eva missed Bobby. They started to become really good friends before they finally made it back home. And she knew Henry missed Amanda.

"I made your favorite strawberry pancakes with whipped cream," Heloise told her.

Henry figured she wanted to send them off on their travels as happy as they could be. He glanced over at her and knew he was right.

"Oh YUM!!" Eva said as she poured on strawberry syrup.

She wiped the syrup off her face when she finished eating her pancakes and drinking her milk.

"So where are we going?" she asked excitedly.

Even if there was danger, she loved to travel. She knew Henry would always get her out trouble. He was, after all, her big brother and he was her protector.

"You're going to an island in the South Seas," Heloise said.

"It's called Tanaka," Henry said. He wasn't going to tell her any more than that.

"Why are we going?" she asked.

Henry realized that he got so

caught up thinking about the headhunters that he didn't know either.

"Yes, Heloise. Why are we going?" he asked.

"There is a princess named Okalani. She is going to be in trouble and she doesn't know it yet. You will need to help her."

"A *princess*? Oooh. Sounds like fun!"" Eva said, happily smiling.

Henry and Heloise just looked at each other, but *they* weren't smiling.

20

CHAPTER FOUR

"Okay, time to pack up and go," Heloise said.

She packed their backpacks with the essentials they would need when they first got to Tanaka - juice boxes, sandwiches and a few snacks.

They always took a little bit of food to tide them over until they could acclimate themselves to their travel surroundings. Then, they were on their own to find whatever they needed while they were there...wherever *there* might be.

They all went into the 'command center' as Henry liked to call it. It was the room where Heloise kept her charts and maps. It was the room where she made her travel calculations and more importantly, it was where she could keep track of them to help *when*ever and *how*ever she could.

Henry sat down with her and she pulled out the travel maps. She measured out the coordinates and plotted their course.

"Okay. All set," she said.

Henry and Eva put on their backpacks and went into the travel circle. First, they said their goodbyes to Heloise. She hugged Eva extra tight... just in case.

They twisted and adjusted the dials on their travel rings and held hands.

As always, the floor began to vibrate slightly. There was a humming sound and a cloud of mist and fog formed at their feet and then rose higher and higher until they were totally enveloped in it. The hum turned into a loud rumble and the floor started to pitch back and forth.

And then they were gone.

24

CHAPTER FIVE

Henry and Eva landed with a huge splash. They landed in water and Henry always *hated* it when they set down in water.

He much preferred to land on dry ground. It was a pain in the neck to find a way of drying off so they didn't have to walk around in wet clothes and squishy shoes.

They waded out of the clear blue water which was at the edge of a huge ocean that went on forever.

They took off their shoes and felt

the sand between their toes. There was bright sunshine and it was very hot.

"Well, it won't take long for our clothes to dry off," Henry laughed.

They were wearing shorts and t-shirts because Heloise knew they were going to a tropical climate.

Seashells and driftwood were scattered all around on the beach. There were lush, green trees with huge bright yellow and orange flowers on them. There were tall palm trees with coconuts surrounding the beach.

Henry was glad Heloise packed their sunglasses so they could stop squinting in the bright sun.

"This is so pretty," Eva said.

Yes, it was, but we'd better get out of here pretty soon, he thought.

They found some huge green

leaves to sit down on and some smaller ones to dry off with. Henry was right. It didn't take very long for their clothes were dry, but their shoes were still a little squishy.

"C'mon, Eva. We'd better start looking around and get settled."

"Okey-dokey," she said. "I can't *wait* to meet the princess! I've never met one before."

"Me either," he said.

He was just hoping she didn't have an entourage of headhunters with her.

They left the beach and made their way into the tropical forest. The trees and bushes were so thick they had to be careful not to get smacked in the face with the foliage. They had never seen such big flowers in so many colors. It was almost as if a rainbow exploded and painted the flowers when it did. There were so many of them and they smelled so sweet, like a hundred gardens all rolled into one.

It was getting thicker and thicker, and darker and darker, until eventually it was hard to see anything. They tried pushing their way through. The ground was soft and mushy and their shoes were starting to get stuck.

"I hope we can get out of here," Eva said.

She sounded a little nervous and reached out to grab Henry's hand. But instead of his hand, she touched something warm and furry...she screamed so loud she scared Henry.

"WHAT? WHAT??" he cried

out.

Before she could say anything, she felt some type of animal jump on her shoulder.

She screamed even louder.

By this time, Henry was at her side and he started to laugh. He reached over and removed a small green monkey that was perched on her shoulder.

When he showed it to Eva she started to laugh too.

"Oh, he's so *adorable*!"

The monkey was chattering away in Henry's arms and then jumped onto his shoulder and back up the tree.

"Oh, where's he *going*?" Eva cried out.

"Back where he belongs, I think," Henry answered.

"Oh," Eva said, disappointed.

They worked their way through the forest until eventually the trees started to thin out and the sun peeked through the leaves.

They heard chattering and looked up. They saw that the little green monkey was following them.

He was swinging from branch to branch and then dropped back down on Eva's shoulder.

This time she didn't scream. She laughed.

"We should give him a name," she said.

"Okay," Henry said. It would be good for her to have a pet on this trip.

"What do you want to name him?" he asked.

"Hmmmm, I don't know. What are some good monkey names?"

"Uh, well, Coco? Churro? Chappy? Chichi?..."

"Chichi! That's it! I like that, Henry. Thanks."

"C'mon Chichi, let's go."

The forest had thinned out and they were entering a clearing.

Henry could see what looked like a village in the distance. Hmmm, he thought, is that where the *princess* is or is that where the headhunters are? How was he going to find out?

They were on a mission to find and help the princess, so one way or another, he was going to have to figure it out.

They heard a slight rumbling and looked back towards the forest. They could see a mountain peeking its head through the clouds. The top of the mountain was glowing red and thin white smoke was rising from it.

"It's a volcano," Henry said.

"Cool," Eva said.

"No, actually, it's pretty hot," he laughed.

CHAPTER SIX

"There!" Eva said as she pointed towards the village.

She was happily unaware that they might be in any danger so she started skipping in that direction.

"Wait," Henry said and pulled her back.

"What? What's wrong?"

"Nothing," he lied. "but I think we need to check things out a little before we let anyone see us."

"Oh, you're right Henry," Eva said.

Sometimes in her excitement, she would forget they were strangers in a different time and place and that they were on a mission that no one knew about except for them.

Henry took Eva's hand and led her away from the clearing and to the edge of trees that led to the village. Chichi was still chattering away on her shoulder.

They crept close to the village. There were many thatched huts positioned in a circle. Women in multi-colored sarongs were sitting near small fires built near their huts. Some of them were cooking in clay pots on the fire. Others were weaving mats and rugs with reeds and grass.

There were children everywhere, running and playing.

"I wonder where the princess is," Eva whispered.

I wonder where the headhunters are, Henry thought.

They stayed hidden, just watching the village. In a little while, they saw a girl about Henry's age. She came out of a larger hut raised up on stone that was set aside from the others. She had shiny black hair and was wearing a flower wreath and a brightly colored sarong that looked very different from the others.

"That must be *her*," Eva said excitedly.

"I think you're right."

She certainly looked different from the other girls and women that were scattered throughout the village.

When the villagers saw her, they

stood up and bowed slightly.

"She's beautiful," Eva said.

She was everything Eva thought a tropical princess would be.

Henry was thinking about how they were going to meet her and find out what help she needed. He didn't think it was wise to just walk into the village and let everyone see them. He followed his instincts that they needed to meet Princess Okalani, alone.

Okalani was wandering through the village and headed in their direction.

Henry pulled Eva down next him so they were crouched further in the trees when Chichi started screeching loudly. He jumped off Eva's shoulders and ran to the princess.

"Chichi, come back! " she yelled.

"Shhhhh," Henry whispered, but it was too late. The princess heard her.

She walked into the opening in the trees and Chichi jumped from her and ran to Eva.

Okalani's mouth dropped open and she gasped when she saw them.

"Who *are* you??" she asked.

Henry and Eva had finally met the princess.

CHAPTER SEVEN

This is perfect, Henry thought. They were meeting her away from the village and out of sight of the villagers.

Now it was time to explain *who* they were and *why* they were there. They had to explain it every time they traveled and it never got any easier.

Whenever they traveled, no one ever believed them at first. He had to find a way of proving their fantastical story to them. Henry didn't blame them for not understanding. If he lived in their world, he wouldn't have believed them either.

Some were easier to convince than others. He was hoping that the princess was one of them.

"Who *are* you?" she whispered, obviously shaken.

Henry knew that it might be easier for her to understand because the only people who had ever *been* on the island of Tanaka were the natives. He knew they had never seen anyone different from them... certainly not anyone like Henry and Eva.

Chichi was excitedly hopping back and forth between the two girls.

"Please don't be afraid, Princess Okalani," Henry said.

Okalani gasped.

"How do you know my *name*??" she asked in amazement.

Well, here we go, he thought.

"Princess, this is going to sound crazy and it might be hard for you to understand."

Okalani sat down on the ground next to them. She remained silent as she listened to Henry explain.

"We come from a different place far away from here."

"But where? And how did you get here? No one has *ever* found this island before," she said.

"Well, this is the part that will sound crazy. We don't just come from another *place*. We come from another *time*."

He was watched her face closely to see if he could judge what she was thinking.

He had no clue. She just sat

motionless, waiting for him to say something else…something that made sense to her.

"We come from the future. We come from a time that hasn't happened in your world yet," he continued.

He could tell she wasn't comprehending any of it.

"There is a whole world outside of this island. A world filled with people and places that is very different from here."

She still sat with a blank look on her face.

This was going to be much harder than he thought.

"We are travelers. We are sent through time to different places to help people that are in trouble. That is why we were sent here. We were sent because you are in trouble."

Finally, Okalani spoke.

"Trouble? I'm not in any trouble," she said, still not understanding what Henry was trying to explain to her.

"If you're not in trouble right *now*, I'm afraid you soon *will* be."

Eva thought maybe *she* could help Okalani understand.

"Princess Okalani, my name is Eva. We have never been sent to help a *princess.* You are the first princess I have ever met. I'm sorry you are going to be in trouble soon, but I'm so excited to be here to help you."

Okalani looked at Eva more closely. She was wearing very strange clothes...clothes like she had never seen before. Both Henry and Eva's hair was very different from that of her people.

Henry's hair was wavy and a color she had never seen before. It was yellow like the noonday sun when it was high in the sky. And it was very short, not like the boys and men in her village. Their hair was long and black like hers.

Eva's hair was brown like the bark of a tree and it fell down like fringe over her forehead.

Okalani was beginning to believe something of what they were saying. They were certainly *nothing* like her.

She heard stories about people who lived across the ocean far, far away, but they had never come to their island.

She knew it must be true. It was the only way she could explain who they were. They were from over the ocean. Okalani didn't know *how* they were able to travel from so far away, but obviously they did. She knew, however, that there wasn't any such thing as coming from another time. She knew that wasn't possible at *all*.

And Okalani knew she wasn't in any trouble, so they made the trip for nothing.

46

CHAPTER EIGHT

Henry knew it was a lost cause at this point to convince her of anything more than that they were strangers from across the ocean. She would believe it when they had to help her out of trouble later on.

He realized that in the confusion, they hadn't introduced themselves.

"My name is Henry and this my sister, Eva."

They both bowed before her because they saw the villagers do it as a sign of respect.

"I welcome you to our island," she said, somewhat entranced by them.

"This is Maru," she said as she scratched Chichi's head.

"Oh, I didn't know he had a name. I called him Chichi," Eva said.

"Maru means friend in our language. He doesn't ever go to anyone except me. He must trust you."

At that, Maru jumped onto Eva's shoulder and she laughed. She felt honored that a royal monkey wanted to be her friend, too.

"May I show you around my island? Then I will bring you to the village to meet my people," Okalani said graciously.

"That would be great!" Eva said.

Henry could see that Eva was completely delighted by the situation.

She was mesmerized by the princess and unaware of the danger that might be lurking. He didn't think it was a good idea to tell her until it was necessary. He was hoping it wasn't going to be necessary at all.

"Let us start with the beach where your boat must have landed."

Yes, we landed…but not by boat, Henry thought to himself.

With Maru still on Eva's shoulder, they headed back to the beach.

Okalani led them back to the beach by a different path. There weren't nearly as many trees so they had a much easier time of it.

They came out on the other end of the beach from where they "landed."

"Where is your boat?" Okalani asked.

"Uh, I'm afraid it hit the rocks and it ripped a hole in the hull and it sank," Henry said, thinking quickly.

Okalani accepted his explanation.

Henry was adept at making up believable excuses when they traveled.

"Oh, my! How are you ever going to get back to your island?" she asked. "I'm afraid we only have canoes for fishing, not for traveling long distances."

"Don't worry," Eva said. "We'll get home."

Their people will probably send another boat for them, Okalani thought. But maybe they won't know where they are. Maybe they are lost and will just stay here with me.

I would like to have some friends.

51

I would like to have some friends who didn't treat me like a princess… because being a princess could be a *very* lonely thing.

CHAPTER NINE

"This beach is called Honu," Okalani said.

"What does Honu mean?" Eva asked.

"I'll show you. Follow me."

She started walking to the water's edge where the big rocks met the sand.

They followed her onto the rocks and when they reached the top she pointed to a small sandy area below them.

"Oh! Henry, *look*!" Eva screeched.

On the beach below, sunning themselves on the sand and flat rocks, were dozens of turtles of all different sizes.

"Honu means turtle," Okalani laughed.

"C'mon," she said and led them down to the turtles.

Some of them remained on the sand. Others were in the water swimming in the clear blue-green water.

Okalani waded into the water up to her knees. A huge turtle swam up next to her and she wrapped her arms around its shell.

Henry and Eva watched in amazement as the turtle swam away with her on its back. Okalani and the turtle went in and out of the water and then came back to the beach.

Okalani let go of the turtle's shell and patted his head. The turtle turned around and swam off again.

"That was *amazing*!" Henry said. "Weren't you afraid??"

"Oh no. Honu Mali is my friend," she said as she picked up a coconut frond to dry off with.

"*Wow*. A turtle and a monkey for friends!"

"Yes," she said sadly. "I am a princess, so I am treated with royal respect by my people. I must act like a princess so I have no one to be my friend except for the monkeys, and turtles, and dolphins, and..."

"Dolphins? Dolphins?? You have *dolphins* as friends?" Eva asked excitedly.

Dolphins were one of Eva's

favorite things. Whenever they traveled to where there were dolphins, she spent as much time as she could watching them swim in and out of the water and listening to them make their squeaking and clicking sounds.

Okalani smiled and walked back onto the rocks. She made a whistling, clicking noise and Eva screeched as she watched a beautiful blue dolphin jump high out of the water and then dive back in.

Then it swam under the water to the rock where Okalani was standing.

Henry and Eva stood gaping as Okalani dove into the water and onto the dolphins back. They watched them swim away, going in and out of the water.

Then they turned and headed

back. The dolphin brought her close to the rocks. She let go and swam back to them.

"I just can't *believe* it! He let you swim with him!" Eva said, barely able to contain her delight.

"Would you like to?" Okalani asked her.

"Would I like to what?"

"Swim with my friend Aku?"

Henry thought Eva was going to faint with excitement.

"*Really*???"

"Yes, she is very friendly and won't hurt you. I will show you how."

Okalani took Eva's hand and led her closer to the water. She clicked her tongue and Aku came to the surface again. Then, he swam to over to them.

Okalani eased Eva in to the water

and Aku swam up next to them.

Eva was giggling nervously. She had never been anywhere *near* a real dolphin. She had only seen them swim in and out of the water.

"Are you…are you *sure* this is safe?"

"Yes, Aku would never hurt you." She stroked Aku's head and he cuddled up next to her.

"Now, Aku, this is my new friend Eva. I want you to swim with her, but be gentle," Okalani said.

Aku made a clicking sound and moved his head as if to say, okay.

Okalani took Eva's hands and had her grasp the fin on Aku's back.

Henry saw both fear and excitement on Eva's face.

Okalani patted Aku on the head

again and he swam off very slowly with Eva on his back. He swam in a small circle several times and then brought her back.

Okalani helped Eva off the dolphin and back onto the rock.

Eva was crying.

"Thank you. Thank you so much. That was the most wonderful thing that has ever happened to me," she said as she hugged her.

Now both girls were crying.

Henry realized Eva must be just as lonely for a friend as Okalani was, but *she* didn't have any monkeys, turtles or dolphins.

She only had *him* and he wasn't nearly as much fun as a monkey.

60

CHAPTER TEN

After the excitement on the beach, Okalani led them to the other side of the island. It was completely different from where they just came from.

There was a very small sandy area surrounded by small green bushes and plants with what seemed like thousands of tiny pink and white blossoms.

Okalani took them through the bushes deep into a wooded area. They came to a tree that was split in two and twisted in an odd way. Okalani took them around to the opposite side...and there it was.

High above the ground, partially hidden from view, was a treehouse, but not just any ordinary treehouse. A small ladder made of twisted vines led them up to the entrance.

Once they went through the narrow doorway, they entered a large room filled with colorful mats on the floor and walls. There were several chairs made of twisted vines. There were green leaves growing through openings in the thatched walls and flowers everywhere.

"Welcome to my royal palace," Okalani said as she twirled around with her arms held out, proudly showing them her special place.

"Oh Princess, it's awesome!" Eva said.

"What does awesome mean?"

"Oh, sorry. Eva meant it's, uh… beautiful," Henry explained.

"I guess we both need to explain the strange words from our languages," she laughed.

"So this is where your palace is?" Henry asked, a little confused that it was hidden in a tree away from everyone.

"Oh, it's not *really* my palace. That one is in the village. This is my special, *secret* hideaway. No one knows about it except Maru. This where I come when I want to be alone."

"Why would you want to be alone?" Henry asked.

"It is very hard to be a princess,

she explained. I can't do what the other villagers do. I can't sit around the fire and listen to stories. I can't play kumo or makala. I can't dance during the festivals. All I can do is sit next to my father, Chief Kanaka, and watch them have fun," she said sadly.

"Here I can sing or dance and talk to Maru and say whatever I like. Here I am free to be anything I wish."

Okalani started to cry.

Henry and Eva looked at each other. How sad, they thought. Eva was thinking that being a princess wasn't as wonderful and magical as she thought.

CHAPTER ELEVEN

Okalani took them back down the ladder. They walked around the beachy perimeter of the island and waded through the warm, ocean water where there wasn't any sand.

It was very hot. Henry and Eva were sweating heavily, but Okalani was cool as a cucumber. This was her island and she was used to the steamy tropical heat.

Okalani stopped at a palm tree and picked up a coconut. She bent down and smashed one end on a sharp rock. It cracked and she carefully handed each of them a half. It was filled with a clear, sweet liquid that they drank eagerly.

Okalani laughed as they swallowed all the coconut water down in one big gulp.

"Thank you," Henry said.

"It was delicious!" Eva said as she wiped some dribble off her chin.

Okalani smiled and waved them on to keep following her.

They ended up on the opposite side of the island on a path that led them to just outside the village. They were near the hut where Okalani came from just hours earlier.

The village scene was the same as it was when they first saw it except this time there weren't just women and children. There were village men with colorful tattoos on their chests and they were carrying nets filled with fish.

Okalani took them through a clump of bushes so they would go unnoticed by the villagers. She led them through the thatched grass door at the back of the large royal hut.

"Please stay here. My father, the Chief, needs to meet you. He will tell me what to do next," she said.

"What to do?" Henry asked.

"There have never been any strangers here before. My people will be afraid."

"Afraid? Of *us*?" Eva laughed.

"Yes. They may think you are enemies and here to harm us," she said very seriously.

Henry never thought of that. They had never been thought of as enemies before, but these natives had never seen *anyone* like them before.

Okalani left to get her father.

"Henry, are you afraid?" Eva asked.

"It will be okay, Eva. Okalani will explain everything to him."

Henry knew, of course, that Okalani didn't understand any of it herself.

CHAPTER TWELVE

It seemed like hours but it was only minutes when Okalani came back with the Chief.

Henry and Eva automatically stood up when he walked in. He was a very large man with a solemn face, carrying a spear and wearing a cape of colorful feathers.

Henry wasn't afraid before, but he was now.

"This is Chief Kanaka," Okalani said.

Both Henry and Eva bowed

instinctively.

They remained silent, waiting for the Chief to speak first.

He walked to the large wooden chair that looked like a throne and sat down. He laid his spear at his side.

"Father, this is Henry."

Henry bowed.

"Father, this is Eva."

Eva stood close to Henry, took his hand, and bowed.

"Where have you come from?" the Chief asked in a deep, formal voice.

"From across the ocean," Henry said.

He had heard stories passed down over the years by his father and his father's father: stories of a world and of a people from far, far away...people very different from them.

The stories told of a people who could be a great threat to them.

The Chief was looking at them suspiciously.

"Why are you *here*?"

Henry looked at Okalani because he didn't know what she told her father.

"Father, they came because they thought I was in trouble," she said, repeating the explanation Henry had given her.

Henry realized how ridiculous it sounded, even to him. How could anyone from 'across the ocean' who had never been there before, know that she was in trouble?

Chief Kanaka rose slowly, picking up his spear.

Henry gulped. He was afraid they were in for it now.

The Chief towered over them in an imposing stance. Eva started to cry.

"Welcome to Tanaka," he said and bowed to them.

Henry was stunned. Why on earth was this royal chieftain bowing to *them*?

He sat back on his throne and spoke.

"You are a shaman," he said to Henry.

Shaman. That was it. He thought he was a shaman.

Eva turned to ask him what that was, but she knew by the look on his face that this wasn't the time to ask.

"Yes, Chief and we are here to help Okalani."

The Chief simply nodded and waved them to sit down on the mats at his side. Okalani sat in a smaller throne-like chair next to her father.

He clapped his hands twice and two native girls appeared from nowhere with trays filled with pineapples, coconuts, berries and other fruits they had never seen before.

They laid the trays in front of them and the Chief signaled them to eat.

Henry hadn't thought about it until now, but they hadn't eaten all day and they were starving.

Silently, the other natives started to come in and sit down in a circle in front of the throne. More trays of fruit were brought in and set before them. They were whispering and eating, obviously whispering about Henry and Eva.

After they had eaten their fill, the

Chief signaled for the food to be taken away. He clapped his hands twice more and everyone stood up.

Henry pulled Eva to her feet. Okalani stepped down from her throne and stood next to them.

Chief Kanaka remained seated and signaled an older native boy, older than Henry, to bring him an ornate wooden box.

The boy obeyed and bowed as he handed it to him.

Okalani nudged Henry towards her father as he opened the box.

The Chief took out a necklace made of puka shells and feathers and place it around Henry's neck.

The natives all bowed to Henry. Okalani was smiling and Eva had no clue what was happening but she figured it wasn't a bad thing.

The Chief clapped his hands again and silently the natives filed out leaving only Henry and Eva with them.

"The Princess will bring you to your kumani when you are ready," he said as he stood up, bowed to Henry and walked from the room.

When he left, Eva leaned over to Henry.

"What's a kumani? What's a *shaman*?" she whispered.

"Tell you later," he whispered back.

Okalani stood up and waved them towards the hut opening.

"I will take you home, now," she said.

Home? Eva looked at Henry. No, they weren't going home. Not yet.

CHAPTER THIRTEEN

Once they were alone in their kumani, Henry was able to explain.

"They think I'm a shaman."

"I figured *that* out, but what the heck *is* a shaman?"

"It's sort of like a fortune-teller. He's almost as honored as the Chief and it's the perfect explanation for why we are here."

Eva had a puzzled look on her face so Henry continued to explain.

"He thinks I can see the future and that I saw Okalani was going to be in trouble. He thinks that's why we came from 'across the ocean'. It's okay that he doesn't understand where we *really* came from."

"Oh, I get it. And this is the shaman's house," Eva said.

"Yup. So it looks like things are getting easier. Now we just have to wait and watch out for Okalani."

When they woke the next morning, they found two native girls kneeling beside trays overflowing with food and flowers at their doorstep.

The girls stood up, brought the food in, laid it down on the floor and left.

They could hear voices outside their hut talking and children playing. Henry stepped out through the grass curtain doorway and everything came to a halt. The children stopped playing, the men and women stopped whatever they were doing, and they all knelt before Henry.

This was going to be much easier than he expected. As long as these people thought he was a mystic with special powers, they would be safe until their mission was revealed and they saved the Princess.

Henry was eager to get things going and hoped they didn't have to wait too much longer.

Eva joined him outside and saw the villagers kneeling.

Henry's right, she thought. The people believed he had magic power.

They both looked up when they heard the rumbling in the sky and saw the top of the volcano glowing red and wisps of smoke rising above it.

"That is Kuahani," Okalani said.

Henry and Eva didn't hear her come up beside them.

"That is where the fire god, Nanakua, lives. He has been sleeping for many years, but we are afraid he is waking up. If he awakens and becomes angry, he will spill fire all over my island and everyone will be destroyed," she said sadly.

She looked back up at Kuahani. The smoke had disappeared and the red glow had dimmed.

"Look," Eva pointed.

"Yes. Nanakua, he is sleeping again," she smiled.

Later that morning, a young boy

of six or seven came to summon Henry
to the royal hut. His name was O'lo and
he was Okalani's younger brother.

"Come," he said, after first
bowing to Henry.

Henry chuckled to himself. He
was never treated like royalty before. He
kind of liked it.

Henry and Eva followed O'lo
through the village. The natives all
bowed as he went by. He had a hard time
not smiling as he passed by, but he knew
he must remain serious as they paid
their respect to the 'shaman'.

Okalani was alone when O'lo
delivered them to her.

"My father is with the tribal
council," she explained. "They are
planning the Nakuahani for tonight.
We have the Nakuahani, a Fire Festival,

to appease Nanakua."

"Oh, a festival!" Eva said brightly.

"Yes, the children string flower wreaths to throw into the fire as gifts so he will stay asleep. My brother O'lo will teach you how to make them," she told Eva.

"What about Henry?"

"No. Henry will stay here to be with the tribal council in the inner circle with my father. Henry, O'lo will take you there now."

"Okay. You will take care of Eva?" he asked.

"Yes."

"Can we go see the dolphins again today?" Eva asked.

Okalani laughed.

"You mean you want to go see my

friends again?"

"Oh, yes, *please*!"

"Okay, but I have more friends for you to meet."

"Really? You do??" Eva asked excitedly.

"Yes. Follow me," Okalani said and led Eva deep into the forest to meet them.

84

CHAPTER FOURTEEN

The sun was obliterated by the leaves of the trees. They were surrounded by thick foliage and fragrant flowers. When they were deep in the forest, it seemed to come alive.

There were hundreds of birds chirping and singing high above them. There were monkeys squawking, chattering, and swinging from tree to tree.

Eva screamed when a snake curled around her foot.

Okalani laughed.

"It's all right."

"But it's a *snake*!!"

"Yes, my friend Tono. Tono, here," she said as she bent down.

Tono slithered up her arm and wound himself around her shoulders.

Eva watched in amazement. Then Tono made room on her shoulder for a large black and orange bird that flew down and perched there.

"This is Loa," she said as she turned her head and the bird nuzzled against her face.

"When I am lonely, I come here to be with all my friends." She lifted her hand upwards towards the trees.

Poor Okalani, she thought. The only friends she has are the birds and animals. At least Snow White had the seven dwarfs.

Far above the trees, Eva and Okalani could hear Kuahani rumbling in the distance.

Henry sat next to the Chief in the tribal council circle. They passed a pipe made of woven reeds to Henry. They had each taken a ceremonial puff from it. Henry knew he was expected to do the same. He took a tiny puff and let it drift out of his mouth without inhaling.

Chief Kanaka dismissed the others so they were alone in the 'healing hut'. It was the place where the council met for tribal business. It was also used as a place of healing when a native was overtaken with an illness or wounded. The tribe's medicine man would bring potions and herb mixtures to drive away the evil spirits. They believed it was evil spirits that made someone sick.

Henry knew that sometimes it worked and sometimes it didn't. They didn't have lifesaving traditional medicine on this faraway tropical island.

Henry was always saddened when they traveled to times and places that didn't have the modern methods of curing simple illness, but he had no power to change that.

"O'lo will bring you back to your kumani and prepare you for tonight's festival," Chief Kanaka said. Then, he stood up and left Henry alone with O'lo.

O'lo was a small, quiet boy who said very little. He stood up and signaled Henry to follow him back to the kumani.

Once there, O'lo removed the ceremonial feather cape from the wooden box he brought with him and placed it around Henry's shoulders.

"You stay here. I will come later for you," O'lo said and left.

Henry waited for Eva and Okalani to return from the forest.

He waited…and waited.

CHAPTER FIFTEEN

The rumbling in the distance grew louder and louder.

"We must go. We must not be late for the festival," Okalani said.

Eva followed her back through the forest.

When they had walked far enough to see the sky again, Okalani gasped.

They could see the top of Kuahani in the distance. There were glowing red and orange flames shooting up and clouds of black smoke rising above it.

"Oh, NO! Nanakua is awake. And he is angry!!" Okalani cried and started running out of the forest and towards the village.

Eva was trying to keep up with her, but she running too fast and Eva started to lag behind.

Just as Okalani was about to reach the clearing, Eva saw two native men reach out and grab her. One of them put his hand over her mouth so she couldn't scream and dragged her back into the forest.

Eva screamed, "*STOP!!*" but in an instant, they were gone.

Eva knew she needed to go get Henry.

She ran as fast as her feet could carry her back to the kumani.

"Henry! Henry!!!" she screamed as she burst through the doorway.

"What? *What*??"

"They have Okalani!" she said, completely out of breath.

"Who? *Who* has her?" he asked calmly. He knew their time had come.

The princess was in trouble.

"I don't know. There were two men from the village that grabbed her. But they didn't *look* like the other men in the village. They were both very, very tall and their faces were covered in red paint. They had spears and..."

"Headhunters," Henry said, more to himself than to Eva.

"Headhunters? *What* headhunters??"

"I knew they were here, but I didn't want to frighten you. I hoped they didn't have anything to do with this, but I guess they do," Henry said quietly so he didn't alarm Eva any more than she already was.

"Headhunters?" she cried. "What do they want with *Okalani*??"

"I don't know. We need to see the Chief, *right now*!"

Henry's feather cape went flying as they ran towards the royal hut. Henry burst through the grass door. The native guard standing next to the Chief pointed his spear at him, thinking Henry was on the attack.

Chief Kanaka signaled his guard to lower the spear. He knew the shaman was not there to harm him.

"Chief Kanaka," Henry said as he bowed quickly, "Okalani has been kidnapped," he said, breathless from running.

The Chief stood and clapped his hands three times. Several men ran in and bowed before him.

"Gather the council. Henry, come!" he said and walked out of the hut.

Henry followed him to the healing hut.

The Chief waited until the council was assembled before he let Henry speak.

When everyone was seated, Chief Kanaka nodded to Henry.

Henry told him in detail what had happened and saw the Chief's face turn pale.

"It is the Maleko," he said in an angry voice.

"Headhunters," Henry said.

"Yes. They are taking her to Kuahani," he said as he banged his spear on the floor.

"Why?" Henry asked.

He needed to know the details so he would know what he needed to do.

"Nanakua is awake. He is angry. We have not had the Nakuahani, the festival to appease the fire god. The Maleko believe that a royal sacrifice will stop Nanakua from covering our island in fire."

"A sacrifice?" Henry asked, afraid he already knew what that meant.

"They believe if they take Okalani to him and cast her into Kuahani that he will sleep again."

Chief Kanaka looked at Henry helplessly.

Henry had told him that the reason they came was because Okalani was going to be in trouble.

And now his daughter was in very great trouble, indeed.

CHAPTER SIXTEEN

Eva was waiting anxiously for Henry to return to the kumani to tell her what the plans were. She didn't have to wait long.

"What happened?"

"The Chief wanted to send out a hunting party for Okalani. At first I had a hard time convincing him that I needed to go alone. Then, I reminded him that I was a shaman with special powers," Henry told her as he twisted his travel ring on his finger.

"You *aren't* going alone," Eva

said. "I will be *with* you."

"No, Eva, I have to do this one alone," he said, knowing she was going to explode.

"*Alone*?? No way!! We are always together and there is absolutely no *way* I'm going to stay here!" Eva said as she stamped her foot on the grass floor of the hut.

Henry had to find a way to explain it so it made sense without alarming her about the dangers of the headhunters.

"Listen, Eva, I convinced the Chief that I could only save her if I was alone. If he knows that I'm not, he will insist on sending the village men too, and that will endanger Okalani," Henry said, in his most convincing voice.

Eva looked down at the floor

trying to figure out a way to change his mind, but she knew he was right.

"Okay," she said. "So what are you going to do?"

He explained his plan in detail so she understood it completely and she nodded her head in agreement.

Good, he thought to himself. She agrees.

"When are you leaving?"

"The Chief told me that the sacrificial ceremony can only take place when the moon is full and that isn't until tomorrow night. That buys me time to find them and rescue Okalani," Henry said. "The Chief is sending his guard with me to guide the way to the Maleko camp.

"Henry, please be careful," she said and hugged him.

"Of course. You know I will be," he said and hugged her back.

He knew he was going to have to be extra careful this time. Bandits and outlaws were one thing. Headhunters were something else entirely.

Chief Kanaka's guard led Henry into the forest on the other side of the island. The guard told Henry there were caves hidden deep within the forest where the Maleko lived. He took him as far as he could without being seen and left Henry there.

Henry stayed hidden until nightfall and was able to watch the Maleko camp without being detected.

He could see Okalani tied to a pole in the center of the camp with her hands and feet bound and a gag in her mouth.

In the distance, Kuahani roared and spewed its flames high into the sky.

There was terror in Okalani's eyes. She knew why she was abducted and what the Maleko planned to do.

Henry waited until the moon was hidden behind the clouds and it was dark enough to go undetected by the Maleko. It appeared they had all gone to sleep since there was no movement within the camp. He crept silently over the grass-covered ground of the forest until he was close enough to toss a rock at Okalani's feet and get her attention.

She looked up and as her eyes adjusted to the darkness, she saw Henry signal for her to be quiet and not cry out from behind the gag in her mouth.

She started shaking her head back and forth, as if to say, 'no'.

He mouthed the words, it's okay, to her, but she continued to shake her head. The closer he crept to her the more violently she shook her head, until it was too late.

He was grabbed by two Maleko warriors and thrown to the ground. One of them held a spear against his chest, pinning him to the ground while the other one tied his hands and feet.

Then they dragged him to a pole next to Okalani and roped him to it. They didn't gag him and they removed the one from Okalani's mouth. They left them alone, both fighting against the restraints.

"I'm so sorry," Okalani said.

"No, *I'm* sorry! I came to save

you," he said, in a bit of a panic.

How could he have been so *dumb* to think the Maleko didn't have guards staked out waiting for someone to try and rescue the Princess? What was he going to do now? He was bound and tied up and could not reach his travel ring for help.

In a situation like this he would be unable to signal Heloise for help.

Henry was truly helpless.

CHAPTER SEVENTEEN

Eva had fallen asleep under a cassava plant after watching Henry and Eva for several hours. She wanted to stay awake, but her eyes just wouldn't stay open.

There was no way she was letting Henry go off without her, so she followed him from a distance.

When he was grabbed by the Maleko warriors, she had to resist the temptation to scream.

She woke up just before the sun rose and the headhunters started to come out of their tents.

Henry and Okalani had drifted off to sleep still tied to their poles, but they woke up as soon as they heard the Maleko warriors' voices.

Okalani looked terrified. She knew Henry was scared but she could see the wheels turning in his head, trying to find a way out of their predicament.

Eva wanted to alert him that she was there and was going to help, but she didn't want to risk being seen by the Maleko.

Eva was only ten, almost eleven, but she traveled enough with Henry to be able to think like him. She knew he needed help. Heloise had not been in touch, so for whatever reason, she was not going to be able to help.

Eva decided that she needed to return to the village and think of something.

Quietly, so she went undetected, she crept through the bushes until she was far away from the Maleko camp. Then she stood up and ran.

When she reached the outskirts of the village, she saw O'lo playing a game with some boys his own age.

He saw her and ran to meet her.

"Where's Okalani?" he cried. "Isn't she with you?"

"No, I'm sorry. The Maleko still have her and now Henry has been captured, too," she said, trying to stay calm.

She knew she needed to remain levelheaded.

"O'lo, I need your help."

"*Me*? What can *I* do?" he asked, amazed that she thought a little kid of seven could help free his sister and her brother.

"Listen O'lo, sometimes us little kids can do things because people aren't paying any attention to us."

"Oh, okay," he said.

Her explanation seemed to make sense to him.

They went back to the kumani for Eva to make a plan. O'lo didn't know anything about *why* Henry and Eva were there or *how* they got there, so Eva didn't need to explain anything complicated. He was only seven and wouldn't understand anyway.

Eva paced back and forth, thinking. She knew that her travel ring was the key to their rescue, but she wasn't exactly sure how.

O'lo watched her pace. Then she'd stop and sit on the floor. Then she'd pace again and sit again. He sat silently and waited for her to speak.

After ten minutes of back and forth, she stopped and yelled, "I've *got* it!"

"Let's go, O'lo," was all she said and he followed her out the door.

They saw huge, billowing clouds of black smoke and fire blotting out the bright yellow sunshine. Eva knew they had no time to spare.

CHAPTER EIGHTEEN

Henry was desperately trying to loosen the cord that was keeping his hands tied behind his back. Okalani just watched him, sniffling back the tears.

The Maleko were paying no attention to them. They were busy preparing for the ceremony they were going to have that night. They were busy preparing to sacrifice Okalani to the fire god.

After an hour of wriggling his wrists, the cord started to loosen and he was able to slip one hand free. He untied the cord, and first looking around to make sure no one was watching, he was able to unknot Okalani's rope to free her hands.

He whispered to her to keep her hands behind her back, pretending they were still tied.

She nodded silently.

Henry was busy trying to figure out what to do next when he heard a rustling behind him in the bushes.

"Henry," he heard in a very faint whisper.

Startled, he turned his head and there she was.

"Eva! What the heck are you *doing* here?" he whispered back.

"I'm here to help you."

"Eva, you need to get *out* of here. *Now*! It's way too dangerous!"

"Nope. Me and O'lo are going to help."

"*O'lo*?" Okalani whispered. "No! *Please* take him home," she cried quietly.

Henry could tell that Eva had her mind set on helping them so there was no point in trying to talk her out of it. He knew his sister was very stubborn, but this time it might actually work out to their advantage.

"Okay. I have an idea. You and I are going to synchronize our rings to take us from the top of the volcano back to the village. I need you to tie our hands back up, but very loosely so they will think we are still bound. When they take us up to Kuahani, you'll need to follow us without being noticed, just in case something goes wrong."

Eva was listening, paying careful attention to everything Henry was saying. They couldn't afford for Eva to misunderstand any of the directions.

Okalani sat, listening quietly, knowing that her fate was in Henry and Eva's hands. O'lo said nothing. He knew he was too little to understand *anything*. He was just happy that he was allowed to be there to help rescue his sister.

"Now we just have to wait," Henry said.

Chief Kanaka sat alone in the healing hut with his eyes closed, praying for his daughter's safety. He knew that the fire god was awake, angry and getting angrier every day. The sky was filled with plumes of thick, black smoke that was beginning to spew flecks of grey ash on the village.

The Maleko were going to throw his daughter into the fiery furnace of Kuahani. They believed that with the sacrifice of Okalani, Nanakua would go back to sleep.

He knew that their own fire festival *might* have done the same thing without having to sacrifice his daughter, but the Maleko captured her first.

Chief Kanaka knew the shaman had special powers and he needed to trust him to rescue Okalani. He told Henry he wanted to lead his village men up Kuahani to help him rescue his daughter, but Henry was very clear that he had to go alone. His daughter's life lay in the hands of the shaman that came from far, far across the ocean.

Chief Kanaka felt helpless, so he just closed his eyes and prayed harder.

CHAPTER NINETEEN

The bright tropical sun was beginning to dip beneath the horizon and the stars were twinkling in the night sky.

The Maleko were starting to chant and dance around the fire. The fiery smoke from Kuahani was getting thicker and thicker obscuring their view of the volcano.

Henry tried to remain calm, hoping his plan would be successful. He knew that if it wasn't, Okalani would be tossed into Kuahani and *his* head

would be hanging on a pole in the
Maleko camp.

Heloise...where are you when we
really *need* you?

Heloise sat in the command
center waiting for a signal to appear on
the travel screen, but no signal came. If
the signals from the travel rings were
blocked there was nothing she could do.
She had no control over the
atmospheric interference that
prevented her from seeing Henry and
Eva's situation. The only thing she
could do was sit and wait...and wonder
if they needed help.

As the night sky got darker with
the black, fiery smoke, the beating
drums and chanting got louder and

louder.

Suddenly it all stopped, and everything was completely quiet.

Okalani looked at Henry with terror in her eyes. She knew what the silence meant. It was time.

Henry looked at her and mouthed the words 'it will be okay' but Okalani didn't think it would be. She couldn't imagine what Henry could possibly do to save her...or himself for that matter.

Eva hid in the shadows with O'lo. She watched as the Maleko lifted Henry and Okalani and headed up the rocky path to the top of Kuahani. Okalani was wriggling and screaming. Henry was quiet because he needed to remain focused on his plan.

Eva and O'lo remained hidden from view, creeping up through the bushes. The closer the Maleko got to the top, the louder their chanting was. They were so involved in their sacrifice ritual that they weren't paying any attention to anything around them.

That's what Henry was counting on. Okalani's life depended on it...and so did his.

He kept watch for Eva and it wasn't long before he saw her face peak through the bushes. He nodded to her and she nodded back. O'lo was hidden safely behind her.

The Maleko carried Okalani around and around in a circle near the fiery top of Kuahani. They had put Henry down thinking he was still tied. They didn't need him for the sacrifice and as headhunters, they would take care of him later.

He slipped his hands out of the loose ropes and untied his feet. He edged his way over to Eva without being noticed and he went over the plan once more with Eva. They would have to act fast, before the Maleko knew what was happening.

Just as in the camp, the chanting suddenly stopped. Henry knew this was the moment they were waiting for. Okalani looked over and saw that Henry was gone and started screaming at the top of her lungs. She knew she was about to be hurled into a fiery death.

"No! No, *please*!! Please, *don't*!!" she cried.

The Maleko brought a special ring of flowers to crown Princess Okalani. They sat her on the ground and placed the wreath on her head. Then, they bowed before her, chanting again.

Henry knew this was the time to make their move. He ran to Okalani and swept her up into her arms. Eva was right behind him holding onto O'lo. Henry signaled Eva and at the same exact time they twisted their rings...and they were gone.

What happened next was a whirlwind of activity. The Maleko watched their sacrifice magically disappear into thin air before their eyes. They gasped and fell to the ground shaking in fear. They saw Henry pick her up and poof, she was gone.

Chief Kanaka had assembled the tribal council in the healing hut and the rest of the villagers knelt in silence outside. They had all heard the loud rumblings of the volcano and seen the fiery smoke that blackened the sky. They knew that Okalani was at the top of Kuahani, ready to be thrown in. They heard the drums beating and the Maleko chanting. When it stopped abruptly, the Chief knew his daughter was going to her fiery death.

He closed his eyes and a tear ran down his face. A tribal chief *never* cried, but he was about to lose his only daughter to a horrible death.

With a flash of light, the rise of fog and mist, and the ground rumbling and shaking, Okalani appeared before him in Henry's arms. Next to them, Eva appeared with O'lo.

The Chief fell to his knees and covered his face with his hands. He could not believe his eyes. Was this really happening? Had the shaman's magic saved his daughter?

Okalani screeched, "Father!" and ran into his arms.

"*Okalani*! You are safe!" he cried.

The members of the council sat in stunned silence.

Chief Kanaka stood up and bowed before Henry.

"You have powerful magic and you have rescued my daughter from her death," he said in a whisper.

He took off his royal cape and place it on Henry's shoulders. Then he led him outside with Okalani to show his people that the shaman had saved their princess.

He raised his hands in the air and clapped them twice.

With that signal, all the villagers including the children jumped up and started chanting and dancing around the fire. They sat Okalani in a woven reed chair on poles and carried her around the fire.

Then all of a sudden, silence filled the air. The rumbling of Kuahani stopped and the smoke and fire disappeared.

"Look! Nanakua *sleeps*!!" one of the villagers cried out.

They all looked towards the volcano in amazement.

Not only had the shaman saved their beloved princess, but he saved their island from the fiery destruction of the angry fire god, as well.

Up on the top of Kuahani, the Maleko were still laying face down on the ground frozen in fear. The princess had magically disappeared and then Nanakua was silenced.

The Maleko knew the shaman came to rescue her and had the power to quiet the angry fire god. They were filled with fear. They knew that never again would they attempt to sacrifice the princess because they angered the shaman and he would certainly return to destroy them.

Back in the village Eva asked Henry what happened to the volcano.

"I don't know, but I'm just glad that it has quieted down, for the villagers sake."

"Does that mean the island is safe?"

"Yes. At least for now it is."

After several hours of the village rejoicing in the rescue of Princess Okalani, they all returned to their huts and the Chief led them into the royal hut.

"How can I ever thank you, Henry?" Okalani asked. "You saved me from a fiery grave."

She buried her face in her hands and started to cry.

"Princess, that was what I was sent here to do," Henry told her.

He knew she would never understand all of it, but she didn't need to. They had accomplished their mission and saved her.

Miraculously, the volcano had quieted down. He knew it could flare up again at any time and destroy the island, but there was nothing he could do about that.

"It is time for us to return home," Henry told Chief Kanaka.

"You have saved my daughter and you will always be welcome here on our island," he said and bowed to Henry.

"Thank you Chief Kanaka," he said and bowed in return.

"I will miss you," Okalani said to him.

He smiled at her and said, "me, too."

It was always hard when they had to leave. They got attached to the new friends they were sent to help.

"I will miss you, too," O'lo said and took Eva's hand.

"Will you come back?" he asked.

"I'm afraid not," Henry said.

He took a feather from the Chief's cape and bent down to give it to O'lo.

"Oh, *thank* you!" he said.

He turned to Okalani and gave her a feather, too.

"Thank you, Henry," she whispered.

She would cherish it forever. He saved her life and he also captured her heart. She leaned over and gave him a gentle kiss on the cheek. He smiled back at her.

"We must go," he said.

She nodded.

Chief Kanaka bowed.

Henry took Eva's hand and they headed back to their kumani.

Moments later the villagers felt the ground begin to rumble and shake and they trembled with fear. They ran out of their huts because they knew Nanakua was awake again.

But all they saw was a mist surrounding the shaman's kumani and then the ground stopped shaking and the mist disappeared.

They were wrong. Nanakua was not awake. It was just the shaman going home.

EPILOGUE

"We're home!" Eva said when they landed.

Heloise was there to greet them.

"I have never been so glad to be back," Henry said.

"I knew it was going to be a hard trip," she said, "but I knew you would succeed."

"There were a few times I thought we were goners."

"You were out of my sight towards the end. I knew you were in danger and I couldn't help."

"I figured that out when we were being carried up to the top of the volcano and I had to rely on Eva to help us get out. But she did it. She came through," he smiled.

"Yes, I helped!" Eva said proudly.

"You did very good, Eva," Heloise said as she hugged her. "I'm glad you made it home safely."

Henry sat down at the kitchen table. Heloise noticed he looked sad.

"What's wrong, Henry?"

"I know we saved Okalani *this* time, but what about the next time Kuahani begins to erupt. The Maleko will want her to be the sacrifice again and I won't be there to help her."

"Oh, you don't have to worry about that. When you disappeared with Okalani, the Maleko thought you were a witch doctor and they fell to the ground in fright. They won't ever bother Okalani again."

"But there's still the volcano that might destroy the island," Henry said.

"Oh, you don't have to worry about that either. You know how the volcano quieted down after you saved her?"

"Yes. It happened just as we returned Okalani to her father."

"Yes, I was watching. When you picked Okalani up in your arms, the atmosphere cleared and I could see what was happening. So when you disappeared, I sent a signal through your rings that put the volcano asleep permanently. They will never have to worry about it erupting again."

"Oh I'm so *glad*!" Eva said.

She was so afraid that O'lo and Okalani's island would be destroyed and them along with it.

"Thank you, Heloise," Henry said. "You're absolutely the *best*."

Heloise laughed.

"You know...maybe I am."

ABOUT THE AUTHOR

Judith Sessler has been writing since she was a little girl of five. She was always writing stories and poems in her school notebooks. When she got older, her imagination continued to create stories to entertain others.

With her love of storytelling, she has written many books for both adults and children. This Travel Kids book is the second in the series with many more to come.

Made in the USA
Las Vegas, NV
13 September 2021

30235629R00085